ALL ABOUT ME

Name: Pippa Jane Saturday Rachel Morgan
(My parents only gave me the middle name
Jane, but I added the other two because I
think it's really unfair that we don't get
to choose our own names. I mean, we're
the ones who have to have them for our
ENTIRE LIVES! I chose Saturday because it's
my favourite day of the week and Rachel
because that's the name of my BFF.)

Age: 10 (which is really cool because ten is
my favourite number in the whole world –
apart from infinity – but I don't think I'll
ever get to age infinity!)

Height: Half a forehead taller than the
hallway shelf. (I know this because I

accidentally walked into the hallway shelf last week and it made a bruise right in the middle of my forehead. I didn't mind though because the bruise looked a bit like the Batman symbol.)

Favourite Colour: Indigo (I'm not exactly sure what colour indigo is – it just sounds really cool. Try saying it out loud and see: IN-DI-GO!)

Favourite Animal: I love all animals, so it's really hard to choose just one. If I had to pick, it would be a bunny-dog (that's actually my two favourite animals in one). A

Favourite Pop Star: Tiffany J!!!

Favourite Song: YOLO by Tiffany J.

Favourite Food: Chicken nuggets and Dad's home-made pizza.

When I grow up I want to be: An acrobatic dancer. Or a spy. Or maybe I could be an acrobatic dancer who spies? I could spy on all the people in the audience at my shows.

swallows back tears Yesterday, at 11.32 a.m., my best friend of all time, Rachel Adams, moved to the other end of the world.

Have you ever lost your best friend? Well, don't. It's the WORST.

Mum gave me this diary.

She said writing stuff down would "help me process my feelings of loss".

???

Writing stuff down is basically *homework,* but here goes. . .

SUNDAY

I can still smell the stink of the removal lorry. Me and Rachel just hugged and cried as they loaded her stuff on. Then I watched like a big-eyed kid who'd just lost her puppy while Rachel waved out of the window of her parents' car.

I will <u>NEVER</u> forgive Rachel's parents – I STILL CAN'T BELIEVE THEY DECIDED THAT RACHEL SHOULD LIVE IN *SCOTLAND* INSTEAD OF THREE DOORS AWAY FROM ME!

Scotland is, like, a gazillion miles away.

Rachel said Nothing Would Change Really. *rolls eyes* She said *We'll still be best friends even though I'm so far away.* I love Rachel but sometimes she can be one fry short of a Happy Meal.

Of course we'll be <u>best friends</u>. But it's not the same. I can only talk to her on the landline. I don't get to *see* her every day.

We can NEVER AGAIN dress up in my dad's extra-hi-vis cycling gear and go and stand under the fluorescent lights in the supermarket and see how many shoppers we can dazzle. The frozen food section was best because the freezers had this cold blue glow that turned us practically luminous. We'd offer to help shoppers reach for fish fingers or ice cream and try not to giggle when they'd half-close their eyes like they were staring into the sun.

We *loved* dressing up. Last summer, we pretended we were characters from *The Lady of Morpeth Abbey* – which was our favourite TV programme EVER. It was *soooo* romantic and

all the characters wore beautiful old-fashioned clothes. Me and Rachel raided every charity shop in town until we'd made the BEST costumes. Rachel dressed as Mr Hunderbentleman (buckle-y shoes and a frilly shirt and a big hat and everything) and I wore ten big skirts on top of each other and put my hair in a bun so I looked like Lady Monteith, and we spent the whole day talking like our characters.

RACHEL: Lady Monteith, may I bring you something from my morning stroll as a token of my admiration?

ME: I would be eternally grateful if you brought me a dozen roses, Mr Hunderbentleman, for my pretty nose needs something delicate to smell.

RACHEL: (*giggling*) My dear lady! Why don't you stroll with me and we may smell the roses together?

ME: Oh, Mr Hunderbentleman! I am so lucky to know such a kind gentleman as you.

And we did it ALL day. Mum and Dad thought it was really funny (Mum and Dad were still married then) and it was the best day ever. Then Mum told us to go and get changed because my big skirts kept sweeping things off her knick-knack shelf and Rachel had to go home for tea.

I wonder what Rachel's having for tea tonight? I could have the same thing and it'd be like we were having tea together like we used to when Rachel's mum went to yoga.

But I can't even text her to ask because she's living on the side of a mountain in the middle of NOWHERE.

Apparently, there are more sheep than mobile phones where she lives now.

This is the first time I haven't seen Rachel for a whole day since, like, FOR EVER.

But Mum always tells me to look for the good things in stuff that happens, so here goes.

<u>Good Things About Rachel Moving To Scotland</u>

1.   Rachel will be able to make lots of new friends (*sob*).

2.   Rachel might get a Scottish accent and then she can become an actor like she's always wanted (you have to be able to do accents to be an actor).

3.   We can write each other actual real letters just like Lady Monteith and her sister, Georgina, which will be really cute.

4. Without Rachel, I'll have lots of
   extra time to spend on homework
   so I can become a genius and
   invent a way for mobile phones to
   text _anywhere_.

I guess I can _visit_ Rachel. Dad asked me where
I wanted to go on holiday next year. Why not
Scotland? There aren't many good things about
your parents getting divorced, but one of them is
that you get TWO summer holidays.

Tiffany J's parents are divorced too. That
practically makes us soul-twins. Tiffany's watching
me now, from a poster on my bedroom wall. It feels
like she can really see me and knows what I'm going
through.

Tiffany J is my favourite person in the whole

world (apart from Rachel). In the poster she looks like Princess Jasmine from *Aladdin* with a floaty headscarf and curly shoes. She is soooo pretty! Who else could look cool on a camel?

She's also the greatest pop star ever. She won the *Voice Factor* last year and since then she's had a billion hits and travelled round the world more times than I've been to school. She's only three years older than me. But she owns, like, fifteen mansions and has a driver to take her anywhere she wants. I bet she has her own pilot too. She must have hundreds of best friends and if any of them moved to the other end of the country, she'd have a zillion new ones lining up along her driveway.

I am SO going to be like Tiffany J.

Imagine if I'd auditioned for this year's *Voice*

Factor. I can picture it now. The judges are sitting behind their big neon desk. Steven Fowl is watching me walk onstage. He has that look like he's thinking, *Yeah, well she's only ten, how good can she be?,* and then I start singing. And my voice is FANTASTIC – even better than Tiffany J's – and when I start my dance, his face lights up like someone's plugged him into a wall socket.

Karen Eastbourne's sitting next to him and her eyes are as wide as an owl's. Then the audience starts cheering me. And standing on their feet. No – they're standing on their chairs they're so excited. No one can believe I'm *that* good! All the judges are AMAZED. Cheyenne stands ON THE DESK and starts clapping.

Huey Brown is pinned back in his chair like he's been hit by a wave.

I wish I could make this happen for real! My life would be perfect!

MONDAY

I'm writing this entry in secret. I have to keep my diary under my desk, on my lap, so Mr Bacon can't see. I've decided this diary might be a good idea after all. I don't know if it's helping me to "process my feelings" but, now I don't have Rachel to talk to, my diary is like my new best friend.

Mr Bacon is teaching us geography. (YAWN.)

He's telling us how mountains are made. *Why?* No one's *ever* going to make one. Where would they put it?

It's horrible being at school without Rachel. Darren's sitting next to me instead. There's playground grit under the desk from his football feet and he smells like cornflakes. I'm trying to ignore him, but he keeps sniffing.

Mr Bacon is drawing a volcano on the whiteboard, firing burning rocks into the air. I hope that the mountain near Rachel's house isn't a volcano. I'd better write to her and warn her to check there's nothing coming out of the top.

I wonder if Mr Bacon is married. He doesn't wear a wedding ring. I guess it's hard finding someone who wants to become *Mrs* Bacon. It's not exactly a normal name. Unless she has a worse name, like Miss Sandwich. ☺ That would be brilliant! Their kids would be Bacon-Sandwiches!

List of Funny Names

Chris P Bacon

Russell Sprout

Justin Time

Stan Still

Hazel Nut

Rob Banks

Jed I Knight

Neil—

BREAK TIME

I'm back. I couldn't finish my list. Mr Bacon stopped drawing volcanoes and started talking about eco-energy. He decided that I should show the class how a wind turbine works. I had to stand up. Everyone started laughing while I helicoptered my arms. It *was* quite funny until I accidentally smacked Darren in the face. He was OK and his nose didn't *actually* bleed. But, even though I said sorry, he asked Mr Bacon if he could sit somewhere else. Mr Bacon said yes and let him move to Tom's table.

I don't know what's worse – Darren's cornflakes smell and football grit or sitting by myself.

They're all in the playground now. I'm the only

kid left in the classroom. Now Rachel's gone, there's no one to play with, so I asked Mr Bacon if I could stay inside and write my diary. He said I could so long as I was quiet while he sorted out the book cupboard. So I'm pretending I'm a spy, like the ones I watched on *Spies Next Door* last night. Mr Bacon is an enemy agent, searching the classroom for state secrets. I'm hunching low to my desk and breathing as quietly as I can. I've made a note of the books he's stored close to the front of the cupboard. They're called *Exploring Japan*. I'm guessing that's going to be our new topic once we've finished learning how to build mountains.

Guess what? Mr Bacon just told me that after break he's going to ask Catie Brown to sit next to me!!!!

Catie Brown is the most popular girl in our year. Everyone wants to hang out with her. She has an actual _ROTA_ for who gets to sit next to her at lunch.

I hope she likes me.

I've got butterflies in my stomach.

LATER

I think Catie might actually like me. 😊 😊

At first she wouldn't look at me. She just sat down and stared longingly at Julie Johnson's table. So I tried doing crazy doodles in my notebook so she'd think I was funny. I drew a talking carrot. And a cat in a space helmet. But she didn't even look at them.

When Mr Bacon told us to colour in our pictures of Henry the Eighth, I told Catie where I lived and about my hamster who died and *all* my favourite TV shows. But she didn't answer, only grunted and coloured her picture in. Then Freya, who was sitting at the table behind, leaned over. She whispered to Catie that she had seen the queue for the *Voice Factor* auditions in town.

I saw Catie's eyes light up and I knew straight away – *she likes the* Voice Factor!

"I auditioned for it." The words rushed out before I could stop them.

Catie looked at me like I'd appeared out of nowhere. "Really?" Her eyes were wide and she was staring at me. "You had a *real* audition?"

I nodded. My face felt bright red but I couldn't stop. I had her attention. So I told her everything, just like I'd imagined it last night. How the judges were blown away and the audience cheered.

And she believed me. Her eyes were popping out of her head, and then she said the magic words.

"You have to sit next to me at lunchtime and tell me all about it."

Lunch was SO scary. The twins, Julie and Jennifer

Johnson, sat at our table. My mouth was so dry I could hardly speak. My mind was spinning as Catie sat down next to me and started unpacking her lunch. I was desperately trying to think up brilliant details to add to my audition story. But the twins kept giggling and started listing all the things they loved that began with the letter J.

Juice. Jenga.

I was trying SO HARD to picture what Karen Eastbourne had been wearing in my daydream.

Jumpers. Jeans. Jelly.

What had Cheyenne's hair looked like?

Jumble sales. Jam. Junior school.

HOW was I meant to concentrate on my story while Julie and Jennifer kept going on about J words?

<u>Things I DON'T like</u> <u>beginning with J</u>

Julie, Jennifer, Johnsons

Then Catie asked me about the audition. "Tell me EVERYTHING."

So I started. "Karen Eastbourne was wearing jelly and Cheyenne's hair was like a jumble sale."

I KNEW I'd get mixed up!

Catie started frowning and I thought *she must know that I'm making it up.*

So I took a really deep breath and started to list as many random facts from my daydream as I could:

My brain started to ache so I took a bite of my sandwich.

Catie offered me one of her crisps. She was all "Wow" and "That's amazing."

I got a wormy feeling in my stomach. I hated lying to her. But it was better than sitting by myself.

Then she said, "I wish exciting things happened to me." And I felt like the biggest liar in the world. If Catie knew the truth she wouldn't want to talk to me. So I said something that was sort of true. "I just wish Rachel had been with me."

And Catie said, "Rachel was your best friend, right? You must miss her."

I was relieved that I could be honest about *that*. I told Catie that I missed Rachel SO MUCH. And Catie told me that, when she moved up to juniors, her best friend had gone to a different school and she'd cried every day for a week.

Isn't that tragic?

We're practically twins (but *not* boring ones like Julie + Jennifer).

Mr Bacon must have noticed because after lunch he paired me and Catie up for our class project. We've got to do a presentation on what it's like to be a ten-year-old girl in Japan. (I am SUCH a great spy! I *knew* we'd be doing Japan when I saw Mr Bacon move the *Exploring Japan* books to the front of the cupboard during break time.) Catie grinned at me as he read out our names and I felt happy for the first time in days.

Then, after school, she waited for me while I got my lunch box and we walked out of the school gates together. Her mum was waving at her from a big blue car.

I stopped as Catie walked up the pavement to meet her. I didn't know if she wanted me following. But Catie waved me over and asked me if I wanted to go to her house after school on Wednesday so we could work on our project.

Her mum was smiling at me through the open car window. She said: "It would be lovely if you could come, Pippa. It's always nice to meet Catie's friends."

Does this mean I'm one of Catie's friends *already*? WOOT!

Perhaps I'll end up being her *best* friend and I can help with her lunchtime rota (I'll *always* sit next to her, of course!). And we can talk on the phone all the time and she'll think I'm way cooler than all her other friends. I can just imagine it now. . .

Phone rings:

MUM: (*shouting up the stairs*) It's Catie on the phone for you again!

ME: (*racing downstairs*) Thanks! (*grabbing phone*) Hi, Catie!

CATIE: I'm planning a party and everyone's coming but I want you to be the guest of honour.

ME: Wow, Catie! Thanks! I'd love to be your GoH!

CATIE: Great! I'm *so* lucky you're my best friend in the whole world.

LATERER

Mum just told me that Dad has found a flat! Yay! Since he moved out, he's been staying with Uncle Pete, but now he's going to have his own place! This means I can stay with him. I like living with Mum but it doesn't seem fair on Dad if I just stay with her all the time. Plus, I miss Dad's cooking. Mum tries her best but she doesn't *love* cooking like Dad does. We've been eating Fridge Surprise *a lot* since Dad left. (Fridge Surprise is whatever Mum can find in the fridge served with rice or pasta. Yesterday we had sausage curry. Today it was cheese and beetroot macaroni. I peeked in the fridge while Mum was washing up. I hope she goes shopping tomorrow because I'm scared what she'll make with yogurt and cauliflower.

After tea, Mum looked tired, so I tried to cheer her up by performing my best magic trick.

I got the TV remote so I could make it disappear then reappear behind Mum's head. But I had my floppy jumper on (the one Gran knitted for me to "grow into") so, when I snuck the remote control up my sleeve, it slid right up and flopped over the armpit-bit and, when I leaned forward to jiggle it out behind Mum's head, it skied down my back and plopped on to the floor. It was like I'd laid an egg.

Mum laughed. So did I. I like doing magic, but I'm glad I've switched to singing. I never got very good at magic. Singing is *way* more fun.

WEDNESDAY

Ms Allen has ordered me to wait in the changing room. My writing is wobbly because it's difficult balancing my diary on my lap while I'm holding my nose. But if I let go (of my nose), I'll choke. It smells like feet come here to die.

I forgot my PE kit. There's no way I'm going to wear someone else's icky kit from Lost Property so I told Ms Allen I'd hurt my foot (which was sort of true because I stubbed my toe on the banister this morning and it REALLY hurt). But then Ms Allen wanted to know *how* I'd hurt my foot and I didn't think she'd count a stubbed toe as a real injury (even though I bet a *real* athlete would – no one could win the Olympics with a toe as badly stubbed as mine) so I told her I'd fallen off the tightrope while I'd been practising my circus skills.

I *know*!

DUMB!

Why did the circus have to be the first thing that popped into my head? There are some BIG downsides to having my imagination.

Ms. Allen looked like she didn't believe me.

And Mandy Harrison was listening.

She said *"Circus skills?"* like it couldn't be true (I bet I could have tightrope lessons if I wanted).

Then Catie stepped forward and said: "My cousin learns circus skills after school at the community centre."

I LOVE YOU CATIE BROWN!

I nodded like crazy and Ms Allen smiled and told me to stay in the changing room. I would

have died if she'd found out I was lying. But maybe I *will* start learning circus skills one day and maybe I will hurt my foot falling off a tightrope. Then it won't be a lie any more.

Oops! Something heavy just hit the gym floor. Jane Harding probably fell off the pommel horse again.

I can't believe that I'm going to Catie's house after school. I'm staying for tea too. Her mum phoned my mum. *Real* food! Mum's yogurt and cauliflower risotto wasn't the best thing I've ever eaten.

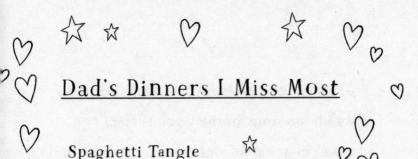

<u>Dad's Dinners I Miss Most</u>

Spaghetti Tangle

Torched Chicken

Tuna Bomb (Dad calls this his
"signature dish" and writes his
name in cheese on the top)

Mausage and Sash (that's what Dad
calls Sausage and Mash)

Pizza Faces (I always choose
pepperoni for the eyes and a
big tomato mouth)

I've just got one problem. Catie wants to hear my audition song for the Voice Factor.

OK, I'm going to confess something, so if you've found this diary and are having a snoop, STOP READING RIGHT NOW, because this bit is REALLY PRIVATE:

I can't sing as well as Tiffany J. In fact, I can't sing at all!

I was the only person last year *not allowed* to join the Y5 choir. I told everyone that I was resting my voice for when I start proper singing lessons (which I'm definitely going to do when Mum can afford it). But really it was because Mr Thompson said I was so out of tune that I was distracting the other singers. He put me in charge of props at our end-of-year show. It was my job to guard the Technicolored dreamcoat while everyone else was rocking the hall with *Go, Go, Go Joseph!*

I refuse to speak to Mr Thompson now. I don't think he's noticed but I always give him a hard stare when I see him. I could be *brilliant* by now if I'd done a year in the choir. Instead I just scare the neighbours. **sighs**

I don't want to scare Catie too. I'm going to have to think up an excuse when she asks me to sing.

<u>Excuses for Not Singing</u>

1. Tonsillitis (her mum might send me home).

2. I'm saving my voice for the next audition (*might work?*).

3. I've forgotten the words (*Catie might google the lyrics*).

4. I bit my tongue at lunchtime and it's too swollen to sing properly (*would Catie ask to look at my tongue?*).

5. I ate chilli for tea last night and

it burned my vocal cords (*she
definitely wouldn't be able to see
my vocal cords – I don't have a
clue where they are*).

6. Steven Fowl made me sign a
    contract promising not to sing for
    anyone outside the *Voice Factor*
    in case I'm discovered by another
    music producer (*that would be so
    cool*).

LATER

I cannot believe what has happened!!

By the time we got to Catie's house, I was so nervous my heart was beating like a drum machine. I felt like I was going to the Queen's house for tea. It didn't help that, when we got there, Catie's house looked like something from a *movie*. The front lawn was practically a *carpet*. The house was perfectly white with a shiny blue front door. The letter box shone like gold. There were no weeds in the garden path like our house. And no chipped paint around the windows.

Inside was even *more* like a movie house.

There were wide wooden floors everywhere. They were so gleamy that I kept expecting a Disney princess to waltz through a doorway.

Catie's mum was really sweet and smiley but, as I walked in, I could see her staring nervously at my shoes. I thought she must have a Fear of Shoes like my mum has a Fear of Heights. Then I saw the gleamy floors and guessed she had a fear of footprints. Catie was already slipping her shoes off so I did the same and Catie's mum snatched them up like she was catching mice. She hid them in the hall cupboard with our school bags and the hall was suddenly neat again.

Our hall is *never* neat. Catie's mum would probably faint if she saw it. There are wellies and coats and bags everywhere (although there's a bit of space now, where Dad's bike used to be). Mum used to joke that our mess hid the stains on the carpet.

ANYWAY.

Catie's mum gave us juice and biscuits. I

thought we'd take them up to Catie's room but we had to eat at the kitchen table. Catie whispered that it was "because of crumbs" and rolled her eyes when her mum wasn't looking. Her mum must be scared of footprints *and* crumbs. (She'd *definitely* faint in our house.)

As soon as we'd finished, Catie took me up to her room. It was HUGE. The size of a netball court with pink and white rugs. And the rugs were so fluffy! I had to take my socks off to feel them properly.

I hopped from one rug to the next. It was like jumping across marshmallow stepping stones.

Then I saw Catie staring at me with big panicky eyes. She looked a bit like her mum.

I froze. Was it against the law to take your socks off in her house?

ME: Sorry. I just wanted to feel the rugs.

CATIE: Really?

ME: They're so soft.

I started to reach for my socks but Catie suddenly grinned and took off her own socks.

CATIE: You're right! They're as soft as kittens.

ME: They're as soft as a rabbit's tummy.

CATIE: They're as soft as the inside of a puppy's ear.

ME: They're as soft as strawberry mousse.

We danced from rug to rug until we were out of breath, and then we collapsed on Catie's bed. And then she said the thing I was dreading. "Do your audition piece, Pippa. Pleaaasssee!" She looked at me like a desperate puppy. I felt hot. I got up and walked to the window and looked out. There was no way I could lie to Catie while I was looking in those eyes. I was just about to explain about Steven Fowl making me sign a contract promising not to sing to ANYONE, when I saw a burglar.

A REAL-LIFE BURGLAR.

In next-door's garden, a big man was heaving a sack down the garden path. He kept glancing back at the house like he was scared he was being watched.

I ducked and flapped at Catie. "Look!"

She came over and looked out.

CATIE: That's just Mr Briggs. He lives next door.

I peeked out of the window. There was a tall wooden fence between Catie's garden and next door's. Beyond it, I could see Mr Briggs heave the lid off a turtle-shaped sandpit. He started scraping at the sand to make a hole in the middle.

ME: Why is he burying a sack in his garden?

Then I remembered an episode of *Spies Next Door* where one of the secret agents buried a load of top-secret files in an allotment. What if Mr Briggs was collecting secrets for foreign governments and hiding them in his garden?

I had to find out!

I rushed out of Catie's room and ran downstairs. Catie was right behind me. As we crossed the hall, she steered me past the kitchen and through the utility room. We charged out of the back door in our bare feet and raced up the lawn.

Catie giggled. "The grass tickles!"

I don't think she'd been on the lawn in her bare feet before.

I told her to shhhhh! Mr Briggs mustn't hear us through the fence.

I could hear him scraping away at the sand.

But how could we see over the fence?

I spotted an apple tree and pointed into the branches. "Let's climb it."

Catie glanced back at the house. "Climb a tree?" Then she looked at her school skirt. "I'll get dirty. Mum'll be cross."

"No you won't!" I pulled her towards the tree. We scrambled on to the first low branch, then the next and the next, until we were peering over Mr Briggs' fence.

Just in time!

The sack was in the turtle and he was covering it with sand.

My brain was whirring. *What should I do?*

I was so busy thinking, my hand slipped and I tumbled round the branch and slid out of the tree. I landed with a thump in Mr Briggs' flower bed. Catie gasped and stared down at me with big owl-eyes. Mr Briggs spun round. He stared at me as I sat among the flowers. Then he looked up at owl-eyed Catie and burst out laughing.

That surprised me.

The secret agents on *Spies Next Door* never laugh.

I decided that he must be *pretending* and jumped to my feet. "What are you burying?" I said, trying to sound calm and strong.

Mr Briggs didn't answer. He just waved Catie down from the tree. "Get down from there before your mother spots you," he told her. He caught her as she jumped and swung her down on to the lawn. "Now what are you doing?" His eyes were smiley.

I gave him a fierce look. "What are *you* doing?" I glared meaningfully at the half-buried sack.

He laughed again.

"Are you working for a foreign government?" I demanded.

Catie stared at me in horror.

But Mr Briggs just laughed again. "I'm hiding birthday presents!" He dragged the sack out of the sand. "For Harry."

Was that a code name for his boss?

ME: Who's Harry?

CATIE: His son

MR BRIGGS: Harry always finds his birthday presents when I hide them in the house, so I thought I'd hide them out here. Harry hasn't played in his sandpit since he was six.

ME: Why should I believe you?

Mr Briggs reached into the bag.

ME: Watch out!

I leapt and grabbed Catie with a squeal. I'd seen something exactly like this on *Spies Next Door*. He was going to pull out a gun and shoot us! I just knew it!

But he didn't. He pulled out a football. And then a brand-new Lego Mindstorms box.

He really was hiding presents!

I started blushing. I stared at my dirty feet.

"I'll get a ladder." Mr Briggs chuckled. "You'll need some help getting back over that fence." He put the gifts back in the sack and headed for the big shed across the lawn.

Catie looked down at her clothes and I felt a prickly worried feeling in my stomach. Her shirt was smeared with green moss and twigs were sticking out of her hair. If her mum didn't like footprints or crumbs, she'd probably *hate* moss-smears and twigs. What if Catie got into trouble because of me?

As we climbed to the top of the fence on Mr Briggs' ladder, I felt sick. Catie wouldn't want to be my friend now.

Mr Briggs called goodbye as we used the apple tree to scramble back down into Catie's garden.

"I'm really sorry," I told Catie. Her mum was staring crossly out of the kitchen window.

I thought I was going to die when Mrs Brown came out of the back door looking like a thundercloud in an apron.

MRS BROWN: (*frowning*) Catie Brown! What have you been doing? (*staring hard at the moss stains on Catie's shirt*) That shirt was clean on this morning!

CATIE: (*staring at her shoes*) Sorry, Mum. We were just playing.

ME: (*stepping forward*) I'm sorry, Mrs Brown. It was my idea to climb the apple tree.

MRS BROWN: (*eyebrows shooting up*) Climb the *apple tree*?

ME: I thought Mr Briggs was a spy.

Mrs Brown opened her mouth but nothing came out.

ME: It's OK. He's not a spy. He was just hiding presents and I promise I'll never make Catie get her uniform dirty again. I'm very good at learning from my mistakes.

(This is actually true. Last year I persuaded Rachel to go to the park, and when we got home, Rachel's mum was all pale and shaky and thought we'd been kidnapped and was about to call the police. We'd been playing Poo Bag and lost track of the time. Poo Bag is a brilliant game where you have to say Poo Bag! every time you see a dog walker carrying a bag with poo in.

Then you score a point. Rachel and me used to play it all the time. When she moved away the score was:

Me: 38   Rachel: 32

I wonder what her score is now? Mine's 45.

ANYWAY.

Rachel's mum nearly died of fright so, after that, every time me and Rachel went out, I always went and told Rachel's mum first.)

Mrs Brown was still staring with her mouth open so I said, very solemnly, *"I absolutely promise that it will never happen again."*

This seemed to make Mrs Brown's eyebrows go back into their proper place. She said, "Well, I suppose it'll all come out in the wash" and went back into the kitchen.

I looked at Catie.

She had her lips pressed together. I thought she was really angry with me, but as soon as her mum had gone, she *smiled*. "That was fun!" *That's actually what she said*. "That's the *best* fun I've had in AGES!"

Then she hugged me!

I can't believe it!

I've made a new friend. ☺ ☺ ☺

THURSDAY

☹ ☹ ☹

Terrible news!

(I'm squashed in a cubicle in the girls' toilets. It's not easy writing in here. I keep banging my elbow on the loo-roll holder.)

The school head, Mr Badger, just announced in assembly that there's going to be a charity talent show at school NEXT WEEK and anyone can enter.

Normally a show would be fun. And I'd get to watch Matilda Sweet from Y6S try to sing harmony with her best friend Jasmine. I've heard cats in the garden with better voices. (They sang "I Wish It Could Be Christmas Every Day" at the Christmas show. By the time they'd finished, everyone was glad it was only once a year.) Some of the Y6 boys always try to be the next big boy band. And the Y4s are so cute when they sing. (In their school assembly last term, they dressed up as fruit to teach us about vitamins and one of the strawberries tripped over and couldn't get up again, so the bananas tried to help him and one of them fell over too and knocked the rhubarb into the scenery. And everyone kept singing the Vitamin Song even though it looked like someone had spilled fruit cocktail on the stage.)

But nothing is *normal* now. I'm in the middle of the biggest lie I ever told. If my Fairy Godmother appeared right now and granted me a gazillion wishes, a talent show is the *last* thing I'd wish for. Why can't I have a Fairy Godmother? I could wish for a voice like Tiffany J's and all my problems would be solved.

Of course, Catie was bouncing up and down as we filed out of the hall. She says I HAVE to do my *Voice Factor* audition song. She says I'll totally win.

I just grinned at her lamely and wished I'd never started this dumb lie. Why can't we raise money with a sponsored walk like other schools?

I can't tell Catie I made up the whole story about my audition. She'll hate me. And she only just started liking me.
She's the closest thing I've got to a bf right now. If Catie stops being my friend, I'll go back to being the loneliest girl in school.

But I *can't* sing in front of everyone. They'll think I've swallowed a cat.

My face is turning red just thinking about it.

Got to go. Louise Hawkins is banging on the cubicle.

BEFORE DINNER

I'm at Dad's new flat. It's brilliant! There are TWO bathrooms, a balcony outside the living room and a nice garden underneath. I'm only staying for tea tonight because Dad has to leave early for work. But I can sleep over at the weekend. I can't wait! ☺

I'm so glad Dad's got his own place. Uncle Pete's house is kind of messy (what Mum calls "bomb-gone-off messy") so Dad used to take me out when I saw him. (Now I know how Mandy Harrison feels. She only sees her dad in Burger King. She says her mum calls him the "Lord of the Fries".) But now me and Dad can hang out like we used to at home. It's a bit bare though, and it's weird that there's nothing in the cupboards and drawers. At home I'm scared to open anything because stuff falls out. Mum keeps promising to "have a clear-out" but she never does. Perhaps she should move into a flat too.

Dad's making Tuna Bomb while I get settled into my new bedroom. "Getting settled" means putting Bobsy on my bed (which took about three seconds), so I've got time to write in my diary. I can smell cheese cooking though so I'd better hurry, Dad will be calling me in a minute and I absolutely, totally need to write down everything that happened at lunchtime.

I could hardly believe it. The twins invited me to their sleepover tomorrow night. (Hanging out with Catie means I've been hanging out with Julie and Jennifer too and they're not boring at all. They don't *only* like things beginning with

J – they like *everything* : cats and rollerblading and hamsters and *Spies Next Door* and prawn cocktail flavour crisps. I think they might be psychic. They keep finishing each other's sentences like they're mind readers.)

So I was really happy when they invited me too. I knew Catie was going, but I never expected them to include me. I nearly choked on my yogurt when they asked me, I was so excited. I thought when Rachel left that I'd never go to another sleepover again. When I get home, I'm phoning to tell her. I wonder if Rachel's made new friends yet. I hope so. Being lonely is no fun. Dad just popped his head round the door to tell me he forgot to buy ketchup. He's turned the oven down and gone to buy some. He'll be back in ten minutes, which means I have the whole flat to myself. I'm going to do my favourite thing – put on my headphones and listen to the latest Tiffany J album. I'll see if I can work out some dance moves to "YOLO", which is totally the BEST track.

It's hard to write with your head under a pillow but I don't care; I'm staying here for ever.

I am SO EMBARRASSED.

I had my headphones on and I was working on the best dance move ever (jumping off my bed into a free spin, heel turn, kick). I was out of breath after twenty of those so I stopped to just sway to the last verse. I didn't even realize I was singing. I certainly didn't know I was singing so LOUDLY.

Then I heard a noise through my headphones. Someone was behind me! I shrieked and nearly jumped out of my socks. I thought it was a burglar but when I turned round, Dad was standing in the doorway, looking pale, with a strange man peering over his shoulder. They were staring at me like I was on fire.

I hauled off my headphones.

ME: What's wrong?

DAD: We thought you were dying.

STRANGE MAN: I was about to call the police when your dad came home.

DAD: Mr Eckington lives next door. (*Dad points to strange man*) He heard you through the wall.

MR ECKINGTON: I thought you were being mauled by cats.

ME: I was just singing.

DAD: (*looking at Mr E*) I'm so sorry we disturbed you. Pippa doesn't usually do this kind of thing.

MR E: Well, that's a relief.

ME: (*blushing so hard I can't speak*)

DAD: (*smiling apologetically at Mr E*) Maybe I can get her some singing lessons.

Mr E: (*smiling sympathetically*) That might

be a good idea. She does seem very (*he pauses while he thinks of a word*) . . . enthusiastic.

ENTHUSIASTIC?

When Steven Fowl tells a *Voice Factor* contestant that they're "enthusiastic" it's code for *terrible*.

I'm staying under this pillow all night. I'm never showing my face again.

MAULED BY CATS!!

What am I going to do? Catie's going to hear me sing one day, even if it's only at the end-of-term assembly. Then she'll know I'm rubbish and I lied about the audition. I wish I could tell her the truth, but she'll never be my friend if I do. I'll be alone for ever.

I wish I was Tiffany J. I wouldn't even have

to go to school. I'd be at Centre Parcs shooting my new pop video in the water rapids. I'd be whizzing down flumes while cameras filmed me, mouthing the words to my next hit as I shot out into a big blue pool. Music would be thumping and everyone would be watching and thinking how cool I am. My personal stylist would be waiting for me at the edge and I'd swim over so she could fix my make-up and start restyling my hair for the next shot. There'd be a whole rack of clothes to choose from for the dance number on the poolside and my choreographer would be working out a new move that everyone will want to copy as soon as they see it.

Why can't I be Tiffany J instead of Pippa Morgan? Her life is way better.

My life is THE WORST.

FRIDAY

Now it's WORSE THAN THE WORST!

Catie put my name on the sign-up sheet for the talent show before registration.

Argggghghhhhh!

She was so pleased when she told me, like she was giving me a present. And I had to act like I was pleased so she'd think I can sing. She mustn't find out I was lying about the *Voice Factor* or she'll stop being my friend. And that would be AWFUL. She's so nice and I feel happy when I make her laugh.

Which reminds me, I'd better smile at Mrs Gould and look interested for a bit.

Mr Bacon is away on a training day so Mrs Gould is teaching us about the Tudors. We've got our exercise books on our desks, so it's easy to disguise my diary as my jotter. I just have to look up every now and then so that Mrs Gould thinks I'm listening.

Mrs Gould is *totally* into Henry VIII. I think she secretly wishes she'd been one of his wives (not one of the headless ones). From the way she's going on about Katherine the Arrogant, I'm guessing she thinks she could have done a much better job as Mrs VIII.

I don't know why *anyone* would want to marry Henry VIII, although it couldn't be worse than being entered for the school talent show when you can't sing.

What am I going to do? If I back out, Catie will know. If I don't back out, *everyone* will know.

Yesterday, Dad managed to persuade me out from under my pillow for some Tuna Bomb. He

said it was OK if I couldn't sing like Tiffany J and
there were lots of other things I was good at.
Like *spelling*, for instance.

Oh, great.

When Steven Fowl ditches *Voice Factor*
and does *Spelling Factor* instead, I'll be fine.
I can imagine the audience standing on their
chairs, screaming with excitement, while I spell
ALGORITHM. NOT!!

He said I could have singing lessons if I really
wanted which was sweet. But even the best
lessons in the world won't teach me to sing by
next Friday.

There must be SOME way of getting out of
the talent show. I wonder if anyone at school
has tonsillitis? I could stand next to them in the
lunch queue and hope they cough on me.

(Henry VIII just executed Anne Boleyn. *SO* mean! At least Mum and Dad managed to split up without anyone getting their head chopped off.)

If I can't find someone to cough on me in the lunch queue, perhaps I can catch a chill by leaving my bedroom window open at night. I know it's only September and the nights are pretty warm, but Gran complains all year about the damp getting into her bones. Perhaps it'll get into mine before the talent show. I can imagine explaining to Catie. "I can't stand on stage. I've got damp bones." Is that why Gran needs a walking stick? Are her bones floppy?

Darren just told Mrs Gould that if he was king, he'd never get married. He said, "Why have a wife when you've got loads of servants?"

Mrs Gould is giving him a hard stare.

Oops, now she's staring at me.

I had to close my diary. 🙁 Mrs Gould told me off for doodling. Doesn't she realize that this diary might be worth a *fortune* one day? I can picture it being auctioned in London . . . *one million pounds, two million pounds, three million pounds, going for three million pounds! Sold!* I wonder how much Tiffany J's diary is worth? I'd give anything to read stuff she wrote when she was still an ordinary schoolgirl. I bet she had big dreams even then. She is *sooo* inspiring. I'm going to be inspiring too once I'm famous.

Quick, there's the bell! There's just time to write this before I join the dinner queue (fingers crossed that there's a cougher)! *Catie just told me that Julie and Jennifer have something REALLY special planned for their sleepover. I can't wait! Squeeeee!*

FRIDAY - MIDNIGHT

I'm at the twins' house, but I can't sleep.

How can I? It has to be the most EMBARRASSING sleepover ever!

I'm curled up at the bottom of my sleeping bag, using my phone as a torch while I write. I'm also eating a cereal bar. There are crumbs everywhere. (It's a good job Mrs Brown's not in here with me.)

The twins are asleep. I can hear their parents snoring down the hall. Catie's bedroll is on the floor next to mine. She keeps giggling in her sleep. She's probably remembering Mr Johnson's face when they finally managed to—

Wait! Let me start at the beginning.

Julie and Jennifer's mum walked us home

from school. She's really nice. She has one of those smiley faces like advert mums, except she's not as skinny as an advert mum and she wears less make-up. She'd brought apples for us to eat on the way home in case we were hungry. (Which I was. It was "sweet and sour chicken" day at school today. I think the chicken must have dissolved because I couldn't find any on my plate and the sauce was so red and slimy it looked like it had been scraped off the scenery of *Emergency Room*. The school chef must have learnt to cook at the same place as Mum.)

Julie and Jennifer's house is more like mine than Catie's and I was relieved that we had to climb over shoes and bags to get to the stairs.

The twins share a room. Why was I surprised that they have twin beds? It must be fun to share a room with your sister – like having a sleepover every night. The weird thing was, Julie's half of the room was really neat and Jennifer's half looked like she'd been burgled. There were clothes all over her bed and books and games sticking out from underneath it where she must have pushed them to make room on the floor for our sleeping bags. We sat in Julie's half and the twins told us about the special surprise they'd planned.

JULIE: Guess what we're going to do after tea?

ME: Tidy Jennifer's half of the room?

JENNIFER: Ha ha. (*not laughing*)

JULIE: Shhh! I'm trying to tell you about the surprise.

Then Julie crossed the room and pulled a scarf off a lump on her desk. Underneath, there's a big, pink CD player.

Catie squealed with delight.

Jenny started beaming as happily as Julie.

I just stared at the CD player, trying to force myself to smile. Lying next to it was a big, pink microphone.

Karaoke!

Noooooooooooooo!

Catie leapt to her feet and started begging to have a go, but Julie said her brother was still asleep because he's working night shifts this week. But he gets up after tea and we could try it out then.

I was still staring at the machine. A feeling of horror was creeping over me like ice fingers. What was I going to do? As soon as Catie heard my Voice of Doom, she'd *know*.

I MUST NOT SING.

My mind started whirling back to my excuse list. Would Catie and the twins believe that Steven Fowl made me sign a contract promising not to sing for anyone outside *Voice Factor* in case I'm discovered by another music producer?

No! There weren't any music producers *here*.

Unless the twins' brother was one.

A spark of hope flashed through me.

ME: (*crossing my fingers*) Where does your brother work, by the way?

JULIE: (*staring at me like I've just asked if she's got a pet elephant*) Why do you want to know?

CATIE: (*squeezing my arm*) Aren't you excited about the karaoke? I can hear you sing at last! It's going to be SO cool. I just hope you don't think I'm rubbish.

ME: (*my stomach has tied itself into a knot even a Girl Guide couldn't undo*) I won't think you're rubbish. (*But you'll think cats are mauling me.*)

I looked at Julie again. "Is your brother a music producer, by any chance?"

"A music producer?" Julie's eyebrows shot up. "He works at the hospital."

"Oh." I stared at the karaoke machine. "I was just wondering."

I tried eating dinner really slowly. Anything to delay the karaoke. Mrs J kept glancing at me with a worried look and asking me if I felt OK while I pushed my peas round my plate.

Catie squeezed my arm and whispered, "Don't you like fish fingers?"

"I'm just not hungry," I replied. I wished the fish fingers were hot enough to burn my throat, but we'd taken so long getting downstairs that they were hardly even warm.

When Mrs J started clearing the plates away, she slipped a cereal bar into my hand. "In case you get hungry later," she whispered. Catie, Julie and Jennifer were already racing upstairs, squealing with excitement. I followed them, my heart hammering like someone was doing roadworks in my chest.

"You go first, Pippa!" Catie was holding out the microphone as I entered the room. Suddenly I knew how Anne Boleyn felt on the way to the chopping block. I imagined the executioner holding out the axe and saying, "Do you want to cut your own head off?"

"No. *You* go first," I told her, trying to sound generous.

She shrugged. "OK."

Catie has a sweet voice. She was watching me nervously while she sang, like she was singing in front of the Queen. When I clapped at the end and told her she had a really nice voice, she blushed. The twins begged her to sing another song and I was SO relieved when

she did. Then they sang a duet. They can do really nice harmonies. It's like *everyone* can sing except me. I must have been cursed by a wicked fairy godmother when I was born. It's the only possible explanation. All the time the twins were singing I knew my turn was coming closer. As they started swaying for their Big Finish, I whispered to Catie, "I have to go to the loo" and rushed out of the room.

Once I was locked in the bathroom, I started sweating. How could I go out there and sing? I wondered whether to pretend I was ill and ask Mrs J to phone my mum. But then I'd have to pretend to be sick all weekend. And I'd miss the sleepover. And they might not invite me again.

I don't know how long I'd been hiding when Catie came and knocked on the door. She said,

"Are you OK?"

I said the first thing that came into my head.
"I'm stuck!"

"Stuck?" Catie sounded worried.

"I can't open the lock." I looked at the old bolt
on the back of the door. It looked like the sort
of bolt that would get stuck, although I can't
remember if it felt stiff when I locked it.

"I'll tell the twins!" Catie's footsteps hurried
away.

I felt relieved for about five seconds. I couldn't
stay in the bathroom all night, could I? I peered
into the bath and wondered if it would be a
comfortable place to sleep. I put the plug in, just
in case, to stop any spiders crawling up.

Then there were lots of footsteps in the
hallway.

A deep voice called through the door. "I'm Jeff," it said. "The twins' dad. Have you tried wiggling the bolt?"

I reached out and pretended to wiggle it. "Yes, but it's too stiff."

"Don't worry, Pippa." Mrs J was calling through the door now. "We'll get you out."

"I don't mind sleeping in here," I offered, half meaning it.

"Don't be silly." Mrs J told me confidently. "You won't have to sleep there. Jeff's going to climb through the window and undo the bolt for you. OK?"

I stared at the window. "But it's too high up!" How would Mr J reach the first floor?

"He's getting the ladder out of the garage," Mrs J called through the door.

Catie's voice sounded beside her. "Don't

panic, Pippa. You'll be out in a minute."

I could hear clanking outside the window.

This was worse! If Mr J climbed through, he'd see the bolt wasn't stuck and know I was lying, and then I'd have to sing, and then Catie would know I was lying.

I AM NEVER LYING AGAIN.

By now, I felt sick and hot. I sat on the edge of the bath while I listened to the ladder creaking outside. Then I saw a shape looking outside the glass and someone knocked on the window. "Open up, Pippa."

I undid the latch and slowly pushed it open.

Mr J caught hold of the frame and swung it wide. He beamed at me from outside. "Oh dear, what can the matter be?" he sang. "One young lady locked in the lavatory." I didn't laugh. I was too busy wondering why even Mr J could sing better than me.

"It's all right, Pippa. I'll just climb in." Mr J was already heaving himself through the window.

Mr J is not a small man. You know I said Mrs J wasn't skinny? Well, Mr J is even *less* skinny. By the time he was halfway through, the window frame was pressing into his belly and he was starting to sweat. His face had turned the colour of our living-room curtains (Mum calls them "mauve" but they're purple).

"Um, Pippa." Mr J sounded breathless. He'd stopped moving. "I think I'm stuck."

I stared at him. Then I stared at the door, which was supposed to be locked. I was totally trapped.

"Mrs Johnson?" I called through the door.

"Is Jeff in yet?" she asked.

"He's stuck."

"Stuck?" (Why did people keep repeating that word?)

Mr J hollered behind me. "I'm wedged in!"

"I told you not to have a second helping at dinner," Mrs J called back.

"You offered," Mr J puffed.

"I was just being polite." Mrs J was starting to sound frazzled.

I backed against the wall, feeling that I was about to be caught in a family row. But Mr J changed the subject. "You'd better call the fire brigade."

Most people might think it's exciting to hear a fire engine come howling down the road and screech to a stop outside. And I suppose it *was* interesting to see a great big fireman appear behind Mr J and start easing him out of the window like someone uncorking a bottle of wine.

But I was mostly thinking about the lock and what everyone would say when they found out that I'd been lying. I made a list in my head about who would be angriest.

<u>People Angry With Pippa</u>

Mr J – because he had to be rescued
by a fireman like a cat up a tree.

Mrs J – because she'd wasted half
her evening rescuing me, then
her husband, for no reason.

Catie – because she realized I was a
liar.

The twins – because I had ruined
their special karaoke sleepover.

My mum – do I need to explain?

So you can imagine my surprise and relief when the fireman (after he'd eased Mr J back down to the ground) climbed back in and reached for the bolt and then <u>STRUGGLED TO OPEN IT</u>.

"It *is* stiff, isn't it?" he'd said as he let me out. Then he nodded kindly to Mrs J and ruffled my hair. "All safe and sound. But I'd put some oil on that bolt. Or get a new one."

Mrs J hugged me. "Are you OK, Pippa?"

I was blushing while Catie and the twins hopped around me.

CATIE: Were you scared?

JULIE: You were SO brave!

JENNIFER: Can I use the loo now?

Mrs J went downstairs with the fireman and, while Jenny disappeared into the bathroom, Catie and Julie dragged me into the front bedroom so we could watch the fire engine drive away. The neighbours were outside, standing under the street-lights, hugging their dressing gowns around them while they watched the fire engine drive away. Mr J was chatting to the man next door while Mrs J was waving to the fireman. I suddenly realized how late it must be.

"What time is it?" I asked.

Jenny appeared in the doorway.

"Ten o'clock."

"No!" Julie sounded upset. "We can't do any more karaoke. Mum said we have to stop at nine-thirty so we don't disturb next door."

I looked out of the window at the neighbours

drifting slowly back to their houses, stopping for a final moment of gossip before they disappeared indoors. "I think we might have done that already."

Then I heard Mrs J's feet on the stairs. "Come on, girls. It's been an exciting night. But it's time for bed."

I looked at Catie, feeling guilty. "I'm sorry."

Catie blinked at me. "What for?"

"For spoiling the evening."

"Spoiling it?" Catie burst out laughing. "You made it the most exciting sleepover EVER!"

Julie and Jenny started laughing too.

"What did Dad look like when the fireman pulled him out of the window?" Julie squealed.

"I bet he looked like our rabbit when it got stuck in the cat flap," Jenny giggled.

I pretended to giggle too, but inside I felt terrible. What would they say if they knew I'd made the whole thing up?

Lying is SO stressful. I'm going to HAVE to tell Catie the truth about my singing.

SUNDAY NIGHT

I had my first whole night staying over at Dadville last night. (*Dadville* is my name for Dad's new flat. Guess what Mum's house is called?) It felt weird to be in my own bedroom even though I'm *not* in my own bedroom. It was like I'd been split into two people in some mad-professor experiment. I kept wondering if, while I was sitting on my bed in Dadville, another Pippa Morgan was sitting in my bedroom at home.

I tried to help Dadville feel more homey by taking two Tiffany J posters – one for my bedroom, one for the lounge (which is actually a kitchen and lounge joined together. Which is kind of fun). Dad said I'd better put them *both* in my bedroom because sometimes he has friends round and it's not cool to be a Tiffany J fan when you're forty years old.

Isn't that SOOOO cute? My dad worries about being cool. He has absolutely no idea that it's impossible to be cool when you're forty.

I pointed out that Tiffany J would probably help him look cooler but Dad told me to put them both in my room anyway.

So I put one over my bed and one over my new desk (Dad bought it specially so I could do my homework when I start staying over longer).

DAD MADE PIZZA FACES!!! ☺ ☺ ☺ I had _SEVEN_ toppings:

Pepperoni (eyes and nose)
Tomato (smile)

Cheese (hair)

Cheese (beard)

Extra Cheese (moustache)

Ham (cheeks)

Sweetcorn (freckles)

Dad even remembered the garlic bread. And we watched a movie. And at bedtime he said I could keep my light on and read as long as I wanted because it wasn't a school night. Mum always makes me turn off the light at nine even on Saturdays!

Having two homes is *definitely* going to be fun.

There was one bad moment.

I was cleaning my teeth in the bathroom and I felt something tickling my leg. I thought it was just a stray hair or some fluff off my dressing gown, but when I looked down I saw that it was a SPIDER.

ON MY LEG!

A _HUGE_ SPIDER.

Of course I screamed and Dad came running and started screaming too. (He's not a big fan of spiders either.) He started flapping at it with a towel while it clung to my leg like it wanted to hug me to death. Eventually, he flicked it off and it scuttled behind the toilet.

Dad _promised_ he'd find it and throw it out before my next visit but how can I be sure? I can imagine it crouching behind the loo, rubbing its

front legs together while it plans its next Pippa-attack.

It's really hard to decide where I like being the most. I like being at Dad's, but then I feel bad that Mum is by herself. But Mum's feels like *proper* home, and that makes me feel sad for Dad because his flat doesn't. It's SOOOO confusing! When your parents split up, your feelings split up too – I have two feelings about everything! Brain-burn!

Dadville vs. Mumville

	Mumville	Dadville
Lights on after nine p.m.	☹☹	☺☺
Pizza Faces	☹	☺☺☺
Spider attacks	☺☺☺☺☺	☹☹☹☹☹
Feels like home	☺☺☺☺	☹
Eating in front of the TV	☹☹	☺☺☺
My own bathroom	☹	☺☺
Mum is there	☺☺☺	☹☹☹☹
Dad is there	☹☹☹☹	☺☺☺
Total	☹ = 10 ☺ = 12	☹ = 11 ☺ = 13

ANYWAY

When Dad dropped me off this morning, Mum had great news. Catie had phoned and wanted to come over so I could help with her dance routine for the talent show.

Catie wanted to come to my house!

When she got here, I don't think she even noticed that our front garden didn't have carpet-lawns and our floors weren't princess-gleamy. I showed her my Tiffany J DVDs and we picked all Tiffany's best moves and worked out a great dance for Catie. She is going to totally rock at the talent show.

After that, I had a brilliant idea. Catie had seen my Tiffany J poster (the camel one) and she really loved it so I offered to give her a Tiffany makeover. We borrowed Mum's make-up and her hair curlers and I found some floaty scarves at the bottom of her scarf drawer.

I'm not exactly good at putting on make-up. I've tried a few times but eyeliner and mascara are very smeary and lipstick seems to want to go everywhere. Blusher is confusing too. Are you meant to put it on your cheekbones or under them? I decided to try both.

The trouble was, Catie kept flinching and giggling when I came at her with the eye pencil. And I don't think laughing when someone is trying to put lipstick on you is a good idea.

I wonder if Tiffany J's make-up artist has to sit on Tiffany while she's applying lip liner? Anyway, I finished at last and managed to get a few curls into Catie's hair without burning her

(though her hair did smell a bit cooked when I'd finished).

I was just pinning on the floaty scarves when Catie's mum arrived to collect her. Catie was really excited about showing her mum her new look. She said, "I keep trying to persuade Mum to let me wear make-up. When she sees how beautiful I look, she'll *have* to let me wear it!" And she went running downstairs.

Maybe I should have let her look in a mirror first.

Catie didn't *exactly* look like Tiffany J.

By the time I got downstairs, Mum and Mrs Brown were staring at Catie as though she had been replaced by a bug-eyed alien.

MRS BROWN: (*turning pale*) What have you done to yourself?

CATIE: (*smiling happily*) Pippa's given me a makeover.

ME: (*apologetically*) We were just trying out a new look.

MY MUM: (*butting in quickly before Mrs Brown could speak*) For *Halloween*. That's right, isn't it, Pippa? (*staring at me with agree-with-me-now-or-else eyes*) They were trying to see how scary they could make themselves look for when they go trick-or-treating.

MRS BROWN: (*looking relieved*) Oh. Well, that's certainly scary, Catie.

CATIE: (*looking puzzled*) Is it?

MY MUM: Why don't you wash it off before you go home, Catie? You don't want to spoil the surprise for the neighbours before Halloween.

CATIE: (*heading upstairs, still looking puzzled*) I guess not.

I went upstairs with her and when she looked in the bathroom mirror I thought she was going to have a heart attack. Mum was right. She looked more like a zombie than Tiffany J. But Catie just burst out laughing when she saw herself. She said, "No wonder my mum looked so shocked. It looks like you paintballed me!"

This made me laugh so much I got hiccups and by the time we got downstairs Mum and Mrs Brown were chatting over a cup of tea. Catie's mum looked really pleased to see Catie back to normal and, after they'd gone, Mum was really nice about her broken lipstick and the eyeshadow I'd got mixed up in her blusher. She said, "It's about time I got some new make-up. I've had this stuff for years. Why don't you keep it to practise with?"

My mum is the best!

MONDAY

Today started off great. If only it had stayed that way.

Catie was practising her dance routine in the playground at lunchtime. She's a really good dancer. I joined in because I know all the moves. Then we showed it to Mrs Khan, the dinner lady, and she looked impressed. Then Catie told her that I was going to sing in the talent show and I'd made it through the *Voice Factor* audition. While I was trying not to blush to death, Mrs Khan asked me to sing for her. Mandy Harrison heard and came to see and before I knew it, Mandy Harrison, David Furnivall, Darren, Julie, Jennifer and Jane Harding were crowding round, all begging me to sing.

Then Mandy said, "If you're such a good singer, why haven't we heard you before?"

I used the excuse I'd used last year about the school choir – that my singing coach didn't want me picking up bad singing habits from a school choir. But all the time, my mind was whirling as I tried to think up an excuse for not singing *now*. Everyone was chanting, "Sing! Sing! Sing!"

It was like a nightmare. So I grabbed my throat and said it was sore.

Catie looked worried. "I hope it's OK for the show." And Mrs Khan came and felt my forehead. "You do look a little pale." Then she took me inside so I could sit in the office.

I'm still sitting here, waiting for the bell to go for afternoon lessons. Mrs Dumpleton, the school secretary, let me go and fetch my diary so

I could write in it while I was waiting.

WHY DON'T I JUST TELL CATIE I CAN'T
SING?

Because I like having a best friend.

sighs

TUESDAY

My lie to Catie has definitely exploded out of
control. *Everyone* thinks I'm going to be in the
Voice Factor. And the dress rehearsal for the
talent show starts in ten minutes.

I'm hiding in the toilets. They are actually a
pretty cool place to write my diary. Especially
now I've found a way to write so my elbow
doesn't hit the loo-roll holder. This is the only
place I can get any privacy. I think everyone
should have their own personal pod at school – a
cosy cocoon with a comfy chair you can snuggle
into, with a soundproof door and a lock, so that
you can hide when you need to escape from
everyone asking you stuff like: *What song are
you singing at the talent show? Is Steven Fowl*

coming to watch? Why didn't you tell us you

made it through the Voice Factor *audition?*

When will you be on TV?

Oh no! Catie's outside, knocking on the cubicle doors. Ms Allen wants the first five acts at the edge of the stage, ready to go on.

What am I going to do?

I know! I'll tell Ms Allen I can only mime today because I'm saving my voice for the actual show.

Brilliant! 😃 😃

LATER

☹ ☹ Stupid!

Why did I think Ms Allen would let me mime? She said, "I'm sorry, Pippa, but we need to get an idea of the quality of your performance."

Catie, Mandy Harrison, David Furnivall and the twins were backstage watching from the wings. Mr Badger, Mrs Gould and Mr Thompson were sitting out front with clipboards, practising being judges.

Suddenly I felt like I was actually at a *Voice Factor* audition, except this time my imagination wasn't going to make everything OK.

Three thoughts rushed through my head:

1. Run.

2. Pretend to faint.

3. Confess.

But as I stared at Ms Allen in total horror, I could see Catie mouthing, "Go, Pippa!" from behind the stage curtain. Then Ms Allen handed me the mic and switched on the tape player.

Time slowed down. All I could do was stare at the teachers/judges while the blood drained down to my toes. I felt so numb I could hardly hear the intro pounding behind me. Catie was staring expectantly from the side of the stage. I had to do something.

So I did probably the worst thing I could have done.

I *sang*.

BIG MISTAKE.

I'm not sure which bit was the most horrible:

1. The look on Catie's face when I
    started (she looked like a fast-
    forward YouTube video, her face
    flashing through disbelief, shock,
    horror, disappointment, then
    anger).

2. When Mandy Harrison and David
    Furnivall burst out laughing.

3. When the twins stared at each

other and said at the same time: "She *lied!*"

4. When Ms Allen told me (using the kind voice she saves for the Y3s) that it was very brave of me to try but I really wasn't good enough to be part of the show. I could be in charge of the props if I liked, though.

5. When I agreed to be in charge of the props (hideous flashback to guarding the dreamcoat).

6. When Catie walked away without speaking to me.

7. When the twins followed her.

My life is totally over.

WEDNESDAY

Catie didn't answer her phone last night. Or reply to my texts. Mum told me to give her some time. She said that Catie was probably feeling hurt that I'd lied to her. (I told Mum everything as soon as I got home from school. She gave me the biggest hug but it didn't stop the awful feeling in my chest like my heart was breaking.) Mum said that, if Catie was the nice girl she seemed, she'd forgive me soon enough.

So when I came to school today, I was half hoping everything would be back to normal.

When I walked into the classroom before registration, Catie was sitting at a different table from the one she shared with me. She'd swapped with Darren so she was back at the twins' table with Freya. I'd be spending the day with Darren's cornflakes breath and football grit again. ☹ I tried to catch Catie's eye, then the twins', and then Freya's, but they just carried on talking to each other like I didn't exist. They all looked so happy and they kept laughing but no one talked to me.

Except Mandy Harrison. She said, "Here's the world's greatest singer! Pippa Morgan, our *Voice Factor* contestant. Come on, Pippa! What did Steven Fowl *really* say when he heard you sing?"

David Furnivall joined in. "He probably couldn't speak because he was too busy laughing."

Then Mandy and David collapsed in giggles.

I hoped Catie or the twins might stick up for me. But they just stayed huddled round their

table with Freya like nothing had happened.

I thought I would dissolve into the floor like a wet bath bomb, but then Mr Bacon came in and started taking the register and then lessons began and I didn't get the chance.

At break time, I couldn't face the playground so I asked Mr Bacon if I could stay in the classroom again and write my diary. Mr Bacon looked at me sadly and asked if I was still missing Rachel. My eyes got hot and prickly when I said yes. Then he said, "I thought you were starting to make friends with Catie and the twins?"

That's when I asked if I could go to the loo because I didn't want him to see me cry. I'm still here waiting for my eyes to stop looking so red. I'd better go and splash some cold water on my face before the bell rings.

LUNCHTIME

I'm glad I've got my diary to write in while I eat.
I don't care if my ketchup drips on it. I'm sitting
by myself, of course. I guess I'm off Catie's rota
for ever. Her table is full. Catie is way more like
Tiffany J than I am, with a gazillion friends lined
up to take my place.

I wish she'd let me explain.

I've tried to imagine this horrible feeling
away all morning. After break I pretended I was
Tiffany J and that I was just visiting the school.
I gave everyone big, happy smiles, and if anyone
whispered when I passed them, I told myself that
they were just whispering about how great I am.

But it's hard to keep imagining I'm Tiffany J
while Catie's sitting three tables away, giggling

with Julie, Mandy and Freya. I bet Tiffany's never been ignored in her whole life.

I'm going to go and stare out of the cloakroom windows. If I'm very lucky I might spot a passing circus; then I could run away with it and never come back.

FRIDAY

Mum's right. Being sad won't make anything better. I'm not going to think about Catie today, even though she's still avoiding me. When the bell went for break, I came to the loo to write my diary. Jenny was checking her hair in the mirror when I walked in and she actually said hi to me and asked if I was OK.

I blurted out that I was really sorry I'd lied to Catie, and Jenny said that Catie was upset because she thought I was her friend and friends don't lie to each other.

ME: I didn't *mean* to lie to her. I just felt so lonely after Rachel left and Catie wouldn't speak to me until she thought I was a *Voice Factor* contestant.

JENNY: (*looking thoughtful*) Why didn't you tell her the truth before the rehearsal?

ME: Because I knew she'd be angry with me and I didn't want to lose her friendship. I really like her. And you and Julie.

Jenny just nodded, like she was busy thinking, and went back to the classroom.

At least I had a chance to tell someone how I feel. I guess I just have to get used to being alone. I'll write Rachel a long letter tonight. I know *she* still likes me. And I might as well try and enjoy the talent show. At least I'm still part of it, even if I'm just making sure everyone gets the right props before they go onstage. I might be so good at it that I end up working in showbiz. What if I was in charge of Tiffany J's props? Or even her *costumes*! I can hear her now: "Pippa, bring me my sparkly dress! And have you ironed the floaty scarves? Really, Pippa, you're fabulous! I don't know how I'd manage without you."

I'd have to go on all her world tours because she wouldn't trust anyone else to look after her wardrobe. Maybe one day I'll even *design* her costumes! Wow! I'd never thought of that before. I bet I'd make a great costume designer! ☺ ☺ ☺

There's the bell. Gotta go.

LATER

That was the BEST SHOW EVER. 😊 😊 😊

    I was standing in the wings with a clipboard, next
to a pile of pom-poms and Darren's ventriloquist's
dummy. I'd already given the Y4s their cardboard
lollies. (They sang the Oompa Loompa song from
Willy Wonka. They were all painted orange.
SO CUTE!)

    I'd held up a mirror so the Y6 boys could check
their hair before they performed "I Love You
Whatever" and I had just given
the Y6 cheerleaders their pom-poms when Catie
tapped me on the shoulder.

CATIE: Jenny told me what you said. (*She
was chewing her thumbnail so I knew she was*

nervous.) And you're right. I did only talk to you because I thought you were going to be in the *Voice Factor*. I'm really sorry about that.

ME: (*panicking because it sounded like she'd only ever liked me because of the* Voice Factor *thing*) It's OK. I mean, you don't have to be sorry. I'm the one that lied and you've been so kind to me and I only wanted to be your friend. After Rachel went away I thought I'd never have a friend again and then I met you and (*I choked up now. It was like everything was washing over me like a bucket of cold water.*) I've been wanting to tell you the truth for ages but I was scared that you'd stop being my friend. I'm *really* sorry I messed everything up.

I ran out of breath. And words. So I shut up and waited for Catie to go back to her real friends.

But she didn't. She stared at me for a bit. Then her eyes started to well up. "Oh, Pippa!" And she hugged me.

Then she gave me a tissue so I could wipe my nose and she hugged me again. Then she said it was OK.

Not just "OK" OK – like people say when they want to avoid an argument – but REALLY OK.

ME: Do you still want to be my friend? (*my heart was beating louder than the music thumping from the school hall*)

CATIE: Of course! (*hugging me again*) You're so much fun to be around.

ME: Even though I lied?

CATIE: You have a big imagination. And you were lonely and feeling bad. And I kind of *made* you lie by ignoring you, which was really mean of me. But I didn't know you then. I'm really lucky that you wanted to be my friend so much because I'm so BORING! But with you, my life is much more fun! I climbed a tree because of you and we're about to go onstage and perform in front of the whole school.

ME: (*my heart dropping into my shoes*) *We?*

CATIE: You can dance with me! You taught me all the moves.

(By now the Y6 cheerleaders had stopped thumping around the stage and were filing past us into the wings.)

ME: (*heart zipping back into my chest and feeling lighter than it's done in days*) You really want me to dance with you?

CATIE: (*laughing*) As long as you promise not to sing.

Then she grabbed my hand and swung me onstage.

Ms Allen stared at us from the far side of the stage like we'd gone mad and hijacked the show. But it was too late. Our music was already playing.

The dance was a bit of a blur but it must have gone well because the crowd cheered at the end. The twins were whooping and the audience were clapping. Then Catie was tugging my hand as she bent into a low, sweeping bow. I bowed too and Ms Allen started flapping her hands in the wings, telling us to get offstage so that Darren and his ventriloquist's dummy could follow us.

After the show, Jenny and Julie were bouncing around us, telling us how great we were. Then the judges announced the winners and guess what? We came second!

I *know*, right?

SECOND!

Then the end of school bell went and Catie's mum arrived and we told her about our dance and coming second and she offered to take us

out for pizza to celebrate.

After-school pizza is the best. Especially when you're sharing it with your new best friend. I was a bit nervous in the restaurant at first because every time I took a bite of my breadstick, I'd send crumbs showering over the tablecloth. But Mrs Brown doesn't seem so worried about crumbs in restaurants and she let us eat as many breadsticks as we liked.

MRS B: I didn't know Catie was a good dancer. She never dances at home.

CATIE: I'm scared I might break something.

MRS B: Then why don't you practise on the lawn. There's plenty of space there. (*she winks*)

Then you could keep an eye on Mr Briggs at the same time, in case he starts burying more things in Harry's sandpit.

I was about to blush, but Mrs Brown laughed so kindly it was impossible to feel embarrassed. Then she dropped me off at home, where Mum was watching a wildlife documentary. I told her all about the show and how Catie had forgiven me and how we did the best dance ever. Mum hugged me and told me I was brilliant, then I grabbed my diary and snuggled in beside her to write while she drifted back to baboon spiders of Borneo.

What an amazing day.

Dancing in front of an audience was EPIC. I can't believe I ever wanted to be a singer.

I still can't believe we came SECOND! And

it was only our first performance. Imagine how good we'll be if we keep practising. I don't think I'll bother being a costume designer now. Not when I love dancing SO MUCH.

I can imagine us at Wembley Stadium. Me and Catie are leading an acrobatic dance company. The crowd are watching us from the shadows while spotlights pick me and Catie out from the troupe. I kick up my heels into a graceful handstand and hold it while Catie leaps up and lands so that she's standing on the soles of my feet. She balances there, then gracefully lifts one leg and pirouettes. I turn slowly beneath her so we're moving like a ballerina pirouetting on a mirror.

Mum's just asked what I'm writing and told her about the acrobatic dance

she rubbed my hair and said, "Your imagination is so big I worry that you'll fall into it one day."

Perhaps I will, but I don't care. My big imagination is one of the reasons Catie likes me. I guess I'll always make stuff up but there's one thing I'll never do again:

I'll never lie to my new best friend, Catie Brown. (Except maybe next week when she comes over for a sleepover at Dadville. I was planning to tell her that he's just staying in the flat while his mansion is being decorated. I like to imagine he's a secret millionaire. I bet Catie will too.)

<u>Top ten reasons why</u>
<u>Catie and I are BFFs</u>

1. We dance really well together — so well we even win prizes!

2. We both like Tiffany J (although Catie doesn't like her quite as much as I do. No one likes Tiffany J as much as I do!)

3. I help Catie do exciting things, like climbing trees and bungee jumping out of helicopters over shark-infested oceans (we haven't actually done that last one yet...)

4. We laugh LOADS when we're together — even when things go wrong. Especially when things go wrong!

5. Catie lives in a perfect movie-style house, but she doesn't mind that my house looks like a jumble sale that's been trampled on by a herd of elephants!

6. We both like walking on tickly things in our bare feet.

7. We do awesome school projects together.

8. Catie actually thinks that my disasters are funny, and she never sighs or rolls her eyes at me like certain teachers I could mention!

9. Catie says that I'm "fun to be around".

10. Catie is really forgiving and kind.

YOLO by Tiffany J

YOLO

You know

So let's go

Have fun!

You only live life one time

So make sure it's a fun time

Join in with this cool rhyme

And come and dance with me

YOLO

You know

So let's go

Have fun!

You only live life one time

So get out in the sunshine

Party till it's night-time
And sing this song with me
YOLO
You know
So let's go
Have fun!

You only live life one time
So make it one long playtime
Join me up on cloud nine
And have some fun with me

YOLO
You know
So let's go
Have fun!

PIPPA MORGAN'S
SLEEPOVER ESSENTIALS

- Your own pillow — other peoples' pillows always feel like they are filled with stones. Why is that?!

- A torch - in case there's an alien invasion in the night and they cut off all the electricity. Or you need to find your sweets during the midnight feast.

- Sweets for the midnight feast.

- NON-CHOCOLATEY sweets for the midnight feast. Chocolate melts and gets everywhere — it doesn't matter how quickly you eat it. One time, when I brought a bag of chocolate buttons to a sleepover at Rachel's, I woke up with chocolate stains all over my pyjamas. It looked très gross! (Très is French for VERY!)

- Your coolest pyjamas — even if they aren't the comfiest. My hero, Tiffany J, says she always wears her coolest pyjamas when she's away on tour. And going to a sleepover is a bit like being on tour because you're away from home and ... and ... yes, you're away from home.

- A Tiffany J CD – she does awesome sleepover music – especially her song *BFFs Forever*.

Shhh! Don't tell anyone, but over the page, you can have a sneak peek at my second super-secret diary:

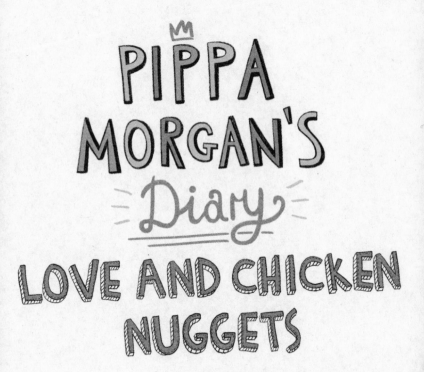

PIPPA MORGAN'S Diary
LOVE AND CHICKEN NUGGETS

TUESDAY 4 FEB

I wanted to start this brand-new diary with some really exciting news, like I've been invited to become a blindfolded trapeze artist for Zippy's Flying Circus, or I've just won the world record for eating the most chicken nuggets while hopping on one leg, or I've learnt how to speak double Dutch. But no. Instead, I have to start this diary with the Most Depressing News in the History of Diaries.

Ever.

Our teacher, Mr Bacon, wants us to do – wait for it – a Valentine's Day project.

Can you believe it???

Blargh!

(I've opened my Exploring Japan book and stood it on my desk in front of me so Mr Bacon can't see me writing in my diary.)

What's so special about Valentine's Day? It's just a day when grown-ups go all soppy over each other. It's full of cheesy movies on TV and icky love songs on the radio. *yawn* And there are the cards. The shops are full of them. They're ALL red and pink and covered in hearts. I tried to find the silliest one in the supermarket yesterday while Mum was choosing vegetables. The top three were:

1. A picture of a pizza with "Roses are red, violets are blue, this may be cheesy but I love you."
2. "We go together like egg and chips."
3. "I love you more than words can say." (I can't imagine ever feeling

anything I couldn't say with words.
Even if it's only made-up words,
like when I feel ickerly-wickerly or
fizzulated.)

Catie just leaned over to whisper that I'm always
fizzulated.

STOP PEEKING AT MY DIARY, CATIE!

OK! (Catie wrote that.)

(I've stood Catie's Exploring Japan book on the
desk between us so she can't see me either. She
keeps giggling and pretending to peep over the top.)

Since my best friend, Rachel, moved away to
Scotland, Catie has become my second-favourite
person in the whole world
(even if she is a PEEKER). We don't agree on
everything though. For example:

my favourite TV show is CopShop and her favourite TV show is Celebrity Gymnast. (I watched CelebGym with her last week. An ancient newsreader fell off the balance beam, and a TV chef got stuck on the parallel bars and had to be helped down. He was dangling over the top bar shouting, "Save me! I 'ave been skewered!" in a really French accent. It reminded me of the time me and Mum tried flipping pancakes and mine landed on the clothes-drying rack and hung there like a floppy omelette. I guess CelebGym is pretty funny, but it's not as good as CopShop.)

Mr Bacon is writing a list on the whiteboard. He's written "Valentine's Day Project Ideas" at the top and drawn big hearts either side with a pink marker! I hope he doesn't want us to write about boys. Boys are annoying. Some of them are OK, but mostly they just want to talk about football and sniff. Boys must have super-weird noses. I only sniff when I have a cold, but boys sniff ALL THE TIME.

Ha ha! Jason Matlock is standing on his chair. Again. He did the same thing last week and Mr Bacon had to tempt him down by promising him he could run round the playground five times. Mum says that some boys are like puppies – they need lots of food and lots of exercise. She says that school is the worst place for them because if they can't run around, they get restless and start chewing on the furniture. Perhaps Jason's mum should send him in with a squeaky toy.

While Mr Bacon is talking Jason down, I can write my own list.

<u>Why Boys Are Annoying</u>

1. They push people in the playground.

2. They eat messily.

3. They talk in class (I write my diary in lessons, but that doesn't distract anyone).

4. They like football.

5. They think burping is funny.

When do boys stop being a pain? I guess when they grow up. Mr Bacon doesn't push the other teachers in the playground. But Dad still likes football, and he used to eat messily and burp until Mum told him not to. Was that why they got divorced? Did Dad want to be able to burp at mealtimes? He's got a girlfriend now. She's called Faye. I wonder if she lets him burp when they go out for meals?

When I know her better, I'll ask her.

LATER (IN THE KITCHEN WAITING FOR MUM TO FRY PIZZA FOR TEA)

I was TOTALLY wrong about Mr Bacon's Valentine's Day project. It's not soppy at all! His whiteboard list was brilliant. It looked like this:

Things you might LOVE to write about:

ANYTHING YOU LOVE!!!

And he underlined "ANYTHING" four times. Best. List. Ever.

So I can write about anything I love! Like fried pizza, or going to the cinema, or Disneyland (where

I've never been but I'm definitely going one day).

This is going to be fab!

The only hard part will be deciding what NOT to write about. I love SOOOOOOOO MANY things!!!! But Mr Bacon says we can only write about three. Only three !

Valentine's Day Project Ideas

Detectives: (like Detective Inspector Mike Hatchett from CopShop.) If it wasn't for detectives, there would be criminals EVERYWHERE!

Dogs: Dogs are the best. If I had a dog, I'd call it Popcorn. I could train Popcorn

to find my hair bobbles – I'm always
losing them.

Astronauts: Imagine floating in space!
By the time I'm grown up, I'll probably
be able to go to Mars. SO awesome!

The Playground at the Park: I've had
some of my best ideas while swinging on
the swings. Flying up and down makes
my brain think better thoughts. It also
makes my tummy feel whooshy and
tickly. I love it!

The Circus: I want to be a trapeze
artist. I also want to be a lion tamer
(except circuses don't have lions any

more. Perhaps I could tame teachers instead).

Tiffany J: She's the best pop star in the world. I was going to be just like her until I realized I can't sing. But I can dance really well, so I guess I could be one of her backing dancers.

Chicken Nuggets: BEST food in the world. The person who invented chicken nuggets is a GENIUS.

Ooh, got to go – I can smell fried pizza burning!

WEDNESDAY 5 FEB

I can't believe I ever thought Valentine's Day was soppy. Mr Bacon's just been teaching us about Saint Valentine, who was really brave and not at all soppy.

He was an ancient Roman and he was like the Roman version of a vicar and he used to marry people in secret so that the emperor couldn't send them to war. Married men weren't allowed to fight because they had families to look after. But the army was running out of soldiers, so the emperor made a law which said people weren't allowed to marry any more.

So Saint Valentine secretly married lots of people (he didn't marry them himself, he just did the vicar-y bit with the "I do's"). But the emperor found out and got so cross that he cut Valentine's head off.

Then Valentine became a saint.

He was SO brave. Imagine wanting to help people so much that you don't mind getting your head cut off. I don't think I could ever be that brave. Saint Valentine is totally my new hero.

I'm imagining being Saint Valentine (before he got his head cut off). I'm marrying a couple in secret. Soldiers are marching up and down in the streets, looking for men to join the army. I'm performing the ceremony in a cellar.

There are flaming torches on the wall and the cellar's all flickery with light. We have to whisper so no one can hear us. I've just done the bit where I say, "You are now husband and wife," and a soldier bursts in and points at the man and says, "You have to join the army!" and I step forward and say, "He can't. He's married!"

That would be the coolest wedding ever. 😊 😊 😊

Mum and Dad's wedding didn't look anything like that. I've seen the photos. They didn't get married in a cellar in Rome. They got married on a beach in Portugal. Which is pretty cool. We went back to the beach when I was four. I don't really remember it, except Mum and Dad stood in the sea and kissed – eew!!

Wow! Mum and Dad used to love each other! I'd forgotten. It feels like they've been divorced for ever, even though it was only

last year. Now Dad's seeing Faye he's happier than he's been for ages. But

Mum's still alone. She's got me, but that's not the same as having a husband.

What would Saint Valentine do?

I know! He'd find her a husband! And if Saint

Valentine can do it, so can I! That's going to be my real Valentine's project – I'm going to get Mum married by 14th Feb so she doesn't have to watch the soppy movies and listen to the stupid love songs by herself. It doesn't give me long – TEN DAYS!!! But if I try really hard, I know I can do it.

I'm going to make Saint Valentine SO proud! ☺